HONG KONG
MOVERS AND SHAKERS

by Jane Houng

QX PUBLISHING CO.

Hong Kong Movers and Shakers

Author: Jane Houng

Editor: Betty Wong

Illustrator: Bianca Lesaca

Cover Designer: Tina Tu

Published by:

QX PUBLISHING CO.
8/F, Eastern Central Plaza, 3 Yiu Hing Road, Shau Kei Wan, Hong Kong
http://www.commercialpress.com.hk

Distributed by:
SUP Publishing Logistics (H.K.) Limited
3/F, C & C Building, 36 Ting Lai Road, Tai Po, N. T., Hong Kong

Printed by:
Elegance Printing & Book Binding Co., Ltd.,
Block A, 4/F, Hoi Bun Industrial Building, Hong Kong

Edition:
First edition, October 2017
© 2017 QX PUBLISHING CO.

ISBN 978 962 255 118 3

Printed in Hong Kong

This book is dedicated to Oliver, Arthur and Tomas.

Contents

Brilliant Bruce Lee Siu-lung

(1940–1973)

Bruce was born in the Year of the Dragon and grew up on Nathan Road in Kowloon. As a boy he was very playful. He would dress in his father's Cantonese opera costumes and play practical jokes on his brothers and sisters.

By the age of five Bruce was already a famous child actor. He skipped a lot of school due to the demands of filming. No one worried about his education because he loved reading books and learned a lot from them.

When a teenager, Bruce was rather

naughty. His secondary school reports were poor and he often fought boys who bullied him or his friends. His father sent him to learn *kung fu*. But he was furious when Bruce beat up the son of a famous gang leader. His father kicked Bruce out of home and told him to make his own living.

Bruce, aged only eighteen, arrived in America alone. He had fifty dollars in his pocket and a sister's address. He achieved independence by finding work which paid for his own food and accommodation. He even paid for his own university education with money he earned from running *kung fu* schools.

Famous American movie actors heard about Bruce and signed up for his classes in martial arts. Some gave him opportunities to start acting again. But Bruce wasn't satisfied. He was only offered secondary roles! Bruce wanted to be the star! After all, he'd already written his own movie scripts.

So Bruce came back to Hong Kong to produce, direct and star in his own movies. *The Big Boss, Fists of Fury* and *Enter the Dragon* were instant hits which broke box-office records and made Bruce a superstar.

Brilliant Bruce's star shone brightly, too brightly, perhaps. One night, exhausted from long hours of filming and strenuous exercise, he collapsed and died. He was only thirty-two.

Bruce Lee dead? Impossible! The whole world mourned. On the day of his funeral, Hong Kong was brought to a standstill. Long may we all revere Bruce's brilliance!

QUICK FACTS

NAME
  Bruce Lee Siu-lung
GENDER
  Male
BIRTH
  1940
DEATH
  1973
CLAIM TO FAME
  Kung fu artist, actor

Enigmatic Eileen
Chang Ai-ling
(1920–1995)

If you were walking along Stanley Street in the 1940s you might have spotted a pretty young lady sitting with a pen in her hand. Eileen Chang used to write in Hong Kong tea houses. She was a master of telling stories about suffering in times of war.

Eileen was a brilliant Hong Kong student who wrote well in both Chinese and English. She wanted to go to university in England but the Second World War broke out so she studied at the University of Hong Kong instead. For three years she deliberately didn't write anything in Chinese in order to improve her English language skills.

Eileen wrote many stories set in Hong Kong and China. Her stories are beautifully written but rather sad. For example, she wrote about her unhappy childhood in her native city of Shanghai. Her father was a drug addict and her parents divorced when she was very young. She also wrote about the soldiers and locals she met during the Japanese occupation of Hong Kong while nursing part-time at a makeshift hospital at Hong Kong University. If you want to know more about this period of history, you may like to read her short stories, or the novel *Love in a Fallen City* (filmed in 1984).

During her lifetime Enigmatic Eileen wrote fictional stories and screenplays from her imagination, as well as translations of popular

English novels. Her writing made her very famous. Some of her books have been made into movies.

In 1956 Eileen married an American screenwriter and they moved to the United States. After he died she chose to live alone again. Some Shanghainese friends who lived nearby kept an eye on her but Enigmatic Eileen was a very private person who preferred her own company, even though many people wanted to meet her. She continued to write right up to her death in 1995.

QUICK FACTS

NAME
 Eileen Chang Ai-ling
GENDER
 Female
BIRTH
 1920
DEATH
 1995
CLAIM TO FAME
 Writer

3 The Father of China

Subversive Sun Yat-sen

(1866–1925)

Sun Yat-sen is considered China's 'Father of the Nation' and the 'Pioneer of the Revolution'. He is one of the few Chinese people who have achieved world fame. Today you can visit a museum in Central, Hong Kong dedicated to his life as a revolutionary. Or you can walk along a historical trail in Central to see the many places he frequented while living here.

Dr Sun was born to peasants in Guangdong and received his secondary and university education in Hong Kong, training to be a medical doctor. But after only a few years' service he decided his life would be better spent curing China from disorder and corruption. Thus, from 1895 he began to plot against the Qing dynasty.

Subversive Sun's work attracted the attention of many rich local businessmen who sponsored him to plan political events. But when an uprising in Guangdong failed, he was banished from the colony by the governor of Hong Kong.

Dr Sun spent the next sixteen years in exile travelling around the world trying to raise money for his revolutionary cause. Meanwhile, agitators in China were proposing to overthrow the Emperor and establish a republic. Gradually these two movements – revolution and reform – merged to become the Chinese Revolutionary Alliance.

The Qing dynasty Emperor Pu Yi was finally overthrown in 1911 and the following January Dr Sun became provisional president of the new Republic of China. The bitter struggle continued and Dr Sun worked tirelessly. When the republic dissolved, the Chinese Communist Party was born.

The last time Dr Sun visited Hong Kong was in 1923. Even though he was only in his late fifties he was already in poor health. At a lecture held at the University of Hong Kong, Subversive Sun urged the students to 'extend England's good governance to the whole of China'.

QUICK FACTS

NAME
  Sun Yat-sen
GENDER
  Male
BIRTH
  1866
DEATH
  1925
CLAIM TO FAME
  Revolutionary and political leader

Saintly Sister Aquinas

(1919–1985)

These days many Hongkongers worry about catching bird flu. Eighty years ago they worried about contracting tuberculosis. Saintly Sister Aquinas spent most of her life treating Hongkongers who caught this deadly disease. Loving and kind, meek and unassuming, she was easily recognisable by her nun's habit and wimple.

Sister Aquinas had a humble beginning. Born into a devout Roman Catholic family in Ireland, she was one of nine children. She did well at school and studied medicine at university where she developed an interest in the Far East. She hoped to do missionary work in China but the country was at war so she came to Hong Kong instead.

Over a thirty year period Saintly Sister Aquinas taught medicine at the University of Hong Kong to hundreds, possibly thousands of students. She also worked for Jehangir Ruttonjee, a very generous Indian businessman who donated lots of his hard-earned cash to build a centre for the treatment of tuberculosis called Ruttonjee Sanatorium in Wan Chai.

Sister Aquinas would become world famous not only for her research and treatment of tuberculosis but also for her rehabilitation of drug addicts. Caring and concerned, this Mother Teresa of Hong Kong provided shelter at a special treatment centre for women who wanted to kick their drug habit. In 1985 she was awarded an OBE by Queen Elizabeth II of Great Britain. But shortly afterwards she fell gravely ill.

A few days before her death a Hong Kong government official visited her in her beloved Ruttonjee Sanatorium. When asked if there was anything he could do for her, she replied, 'Please take good care of my drug addicts.'

QUICK FACTS

NAME
Sister Aquinas
GENDER
Female
BIRTH
1919
DEATH
1985
CLAIM TO FAME
Physician and clinical lecturer. Rehabilitator of drug-addicts

Conscientious Catherine
Symons
(1918–2004)

Catherine Symons was half British, half Chinese: a Eurasian. She described herself as 'the blood of Old China mixed with that of Europe'. She was the third of five children. Her grandfather had been a translator at the Supreme Court. Conscientious Catherine studied hard at school and achieved excellent results. She grew into a beautiful woman with black hair and dark eyes.

From a very early age Catherine knew she wanted to be a teacher. After graduating from the University of Hong Kong, she taught at Diocesan Girls' School (DGS). But when Japan invaded Hong Kong in 1941 the school closed and she moved with her family to Macau. They would have preferred to evacuate to Australia but couldn't get a visa due to their mixed blood.

DGS was used by the Japanese to house soldiers who doubled up as police: the 'gendarmerie'. After the war, Catherine returned to work there, and in 1953 became the headmistress – the first Eurasian to hold this post. She would be the headmistress for over thirty years and under her leadership, DGS became one of the most competitive elite girls' schools in Hong Kong.

Conscientious Catherine cared for all her pupils very much and worked hard to instil the 'five pillars' of a DGS education: steadfastness in learning, sensitivity towards beauty, stamina for sports, generosity in service, and the nurturing of a spiritual life.

Catherine was also very active in public service. She was a very outspoken woman who championed women's rights. She served on the Urban Council and the Legislative Council. In 1976 she was appointed to the Executive Council, making her the first woman to hold such a prestigious position.

Her husband, also a Eurasian, worked as a doctor. In 1985 they retired and emigrated to the United Kingdom, the birthplace of their European ancestors.

QUICK FACTS

NAME
  Catherine Symons
GENDER
  Female
BIRTH
  1918
DEATH
  2004
CLAIM TO FAME
  Educator

An Anti-foot-binding Campaigner

Amazing Alicia Little

(1845–1926)

For thousands of years many middle- and upper-class Han Chinese girls had broken feet. Their toes were tucked underneath the soles of their feet and tightly bound inside doll-sized shoes. That's because small feet ('three-inch golden lilies') were considered a mark of beauty and a symbol of men's power over women. But the process was very painful and made feet smell like rotting flesh. Besides, the poor girls were unable to walk properly, never mind hop, skip, or play. They then had to spend their adult lives at home being waited on by servants. Can you believe that the tradition of foot binding didn't die out until the early twentieth century?

Amazing Alicia was little in caution and big on ambition. What was her dream? To persuade people that foot binding was cruel and ugly. While based in Shanghai with her husband, a tea taster, she put her life in danger by travelling around China campaigning against the practice and arguing with local officials and scholars.

In 1900 Alicia came to Hong Kong to speak at the Chinese Club. She also lectured at Queen's College where she encouraged five hundred young men to consider marrying girls without fashionable bound feet. On another trip she organised a meeting at Government House targeting local Chinese women, and persuaded forty-seven of them to sign up as members of her Natural Feet Society.

Amazing Alicia retired in England where she wrote *In the Land of the Blue Gown*. The book shows that with energy and determination you can make your dreams come true.

QUICK FACTS

NAME
  Alicia Little
GENDER
  Female
BIRTH
  1845
DEATH
  1926
CLAIM TO FAME
  Writer, campaigner against foot binding

Daring Daniel Caldwell

(1816–1875)

D aniel Caldwell's tombstone is one of the tallest in Happy Valley cemetery. Who was he? Why do some people say he was a turncoat?

Daniel was born on Saint Helena, a small tropical island in the South Atlantic Ocean. He arrived in Hong Kong in 1842, the first year of the British colony. It was a time of war, piracy, corruption and political scandal. Daniel quickly learned several Chinese dialects, as well as Malay, Hindustani and Portuguese.

These language skills made him very useful to the new colonial government. He tracked down wanted criminals, captured pirates, discovered spies, uncovered plots and advised on the sentiment of the Chinese community. Many locals resented being governed by an alien power. One morning in 1857, for example, bakers hoping to kill all non-Chinese laced their bread with poison. But they added so much arsenic that people vomited the bread up instead.

Daring Daniel relied on Chinese informants for his valuable information. This eventually caused him to be accused of corruption. He was sent to court to defend his good character, where the lawyers accused him of being immoral. Why? Because he was married to a local Chinese lady, the first mixed marriage recorded in Hong Kong. In reality, Daniel's marriage was a very happy one. He and his wife were Christians. They had at least eight children and fostered another twenty during their lifetime together.

As a result of the court case, Daniel lost all his government positions. Instead he made his living as a Chinese agent for Hong Kong businessmen. Still later in his career he worked for the British government again, this time as the head of the secret police.

What a colourful life Daring Daniel led!

QUICK FACTS

NAME

 Daniel Caldwell

GENDER

 Male

BIRTH

 1816

DEATH

 1875

CLAIM TO FAME

 Colonial officer, interpreter, policeman and Chinese agent

Patient Patrick Manson

(1844–1922)

D octor Manson was a parasitologist. What's that? you may ask. It's someone who studies parasites, those pesky organisms that feed on us, like tapeworms, fleas, ticks and mosquitoes.

Doctor Manson was Scottish and worked as a doctor in Asia. He was a founding member of the College of Medicine for Chinese in Hong Kong, which later became the medical faculty of the University of Hong Kong. He had business interests too. With several local businessmen he set up a dairy farm in Pok Fu Lam in order to breed cattle and supply fresh milk to the territory. This farm later became the Dairy Farm Company.

Patient Patrick had a special interest in mosquitoes and a hunch that their bites could cause disease. But it took him many years of research to make his major breakthrough. While working in Formosa (present-day Taiwan) he proved they were responsible for causing elephantiasis – an ugly condition that eventually makes you look like … an elephant. Then in Hong Kong between 1883 and 1889, when doctors couldn't distinguish between typhoid and malaria, he began researching into what made these two diseases different.

Doctor Manson returned to Britain in 1889 where he worked at a seamen's hospital and treated all kinds of tropical diseases. It was there that he published a paper proposing that malaria was transmitted by mosquitoes. Some of his colleagues weren't convinced. So in 1900 he conducted an experiment to prove it, releasing hungry mosquitoes to feed on his son! Sure enough, within fifteen days the parasites could clearly be seen in his son's blood.

For this discovery, Doctor Manson was awarded an honorary doctorate from Oxford University. He was also awarded a GCMG (Great Britain's highest order of chivalry) and became a 'Sir'.

Sir Patrick retired to Ireland and spent his old age fishing. He's now remembered as 'the Father of Tropical Diseases'.

QUICK FACTS

NAME

Sir Patrick Manson

GENDER

Male

BIRTH

1844

DEATH

1922

CLAIM TO FAME

Parasitologist who discovered that mosquitoes caused malaria

Dastardly Du Yuesheng

(1888–1951)

Some people become famous for being very, very good. Others become infamous for being very, very bad. The Chinese gangster Du Yuesheng was infamous. Orphaned when only nine, he started working in the opium and gambling area of Shanghai. By the age of sixteen he was a member of the Green Gang, a secret society which controlled the criminal activities in the city.

Dastardly Du soon became mob boss by establishing relationships with corrupt policemen in the French Concession area of Shanghai. Nicknamed 'Big-eared Du', he had three small monkey heads sewn into the back of his coat for good luck. Dastardly Du was never short of money. He traded with the high end of society – warlords, police, French authorities – as well as factory workers, transport workers and beggars. To hide his criminal activities he opened legal practices, founded a bank and at one stage was the director of both the Shanghai Stock Exchange and the Shanghai Bankers Association.

How did Du like to spend his free time? Watching Peking opera. He would book the best seats of the theatres, surround himself with White Russian bodyguards and eat and drink and sing. He adored the colour, drama and spectacle of the operas and could recite all the famous ones by heart.

Dastardly Du relocated to Hong Kong when

the communists took control over Shanghai in 1949. To keep him company, he brought family members, gambling friends, Peking opera singers and other Shanghainese exiles. But his plan to enjoy a comfortable life here was marred by ill health. He was hopelessly addicted to opium and suffered from chronic asthma. When he died at the age of sixty-one, lavish funeral rites were held at the Luk Kwok Hotel in Wan Chai.

QUICK FACTS

NAME
  Du Yuesheng
GENDER
  Male
BIRTH
  1888
DEATH
  1951
CLAIM TO FAME
  Gangster

Generous Jehangir Ruttonjee

(1880–1960)

The most generous philanthropist in early twentieth-century Hong Kong was an Indian immigrant called Jehangir Ruttonjee. Buildings constructed by his initiative and generosity can still be seen in Hong Kong. There's the Ruttonjee Centre in Central, for example, as well as Ruttonjee Hospital and Grantham Hospital.

Jehangir's family was Parsee, a religious group that moved from Persia to India and East Asia after being persecuted by Muslims.

There are still Parsees living in Hong Kong today and they have played a significant part in the city's development.

Jehangir was twelve when he came to Hong Kong. His father was a wine, spirit and food trader here. Jehangir worked hard at school then joined his father's business. A few years later he founded his own beer company on Castle Peak Road and started buying property. Soon he was rich.

But his life took an unfortunate turn during the Japanese occupation. When the Japanese discovered that he was offering free goods and shelter to desperate local people in Dina House and Ruttonjee Building he was thrown into prison for three years. While imprisoned, one of his beloved daughters died of tuberculosis. One of the first things Generous Jehangir did after the war was to gift $500,000 for the building of a hospital that specialised in fighting this often fatal disease. In Hong Kong's history it was the biggest gift ever from any person or institution. At the opening of Ruttonjee Sanatorium in 1944 he said: 'Whatever our race and whatever our religious belief, our common humanity demands our help for the needy and suffering around us.'

In 1953 tragedy struck again: his second daughter died of cancer. That's when Jehangir made a large donation to build Freni Memorial Convalescent Home in Stubbs Road. He also contributed over two million dollars to build Grantham Hospital.

After Generous Jehangir's death in 1960, his son continued his father's fine family tradition of philanthropy.

QUICK FACTS

NAME
 Jehangir Ruttonjee
GENDER
 Male
BIRTH
 1880
DEATH
 1960
CLAIM TO FAME
 Entrepreneur and philanthropist

Luckless Lai Man-wai

(1893–1953)

At Lai Man-wai's funeral in 1953 a big banner hung above his coffin. It read: 'Father of Hong Kong Cinema'. Who was this man? How did he become so famous?

The illustration on Page 44 shows Mr Lai in 1913. He's acting in the first movie ever made in Hong Kong: *Zhuangzi Tests His Wife*. Why on earth is he wearing a dress? He looks like a woman, right? That's because he was playing the part of Zhuangzi's wife. In those days, all women's roles were played by men!

Luckless Lai studied in Hong Kong where he developed an interest in photography and drama. During his career he set up movie companies in Hong Kong and Shanghai. But he lived in times of great political change and lost lots of money on his productions. For example, in 1936 he registered the China Sun Motion Picture Production Company in Shanghai but was forced to close it a year later because of the Japanese invasion. Then in 1941, while back living in Hong Kong, he founded a film studio called Qiming. But within months the Japanese were invading here too. Luckless Lai fled with his two wives and twelve children to China.

Lai Man-wai wrote a diary in which you can read more about his colourful life. After the Japanese surrender he came back to Hong Kong and, in order to support his large family, set up a small film-processing studio.

Shortly before he died, Luckless Lai wrote down his life teachings. They are:

i. Don't speculate. It can bring both success and failure;

ii. Making money is detrimental to living a meaningful life;

iii. Don't get involved in politics or the military;

iv. You won't have any burdens if you don't expect any returns for doing favours for others.

QUICK FACTS

NAME

Lai Man-wai

GENDER

Male

BIRTH

1893

DEATH

1953

CLAIM TO FAME

Father of Hong Kong cinema

Revered Reverend Carl Smith
(1918–2008)

It's very convenient to research for school projects these days, right? Surf the internet, one click here, another there, and you have tons of information. Often too much. How did people do research in the olden days? Mostly by word-of-mouth and reading books. But reading materials about early Hong Kong history gave researchers a very one-sided view. Practically all the documents – government reports, court documents, newspapers – were written from a colonial perspective. Virtually nothing was recorded from the viewpoint of local Chinese. That all changed when Reverend Carl Smith moved from America to Hong Kong in 1960 and began to work at the Hong Kong Council for the Church of Christ.

Soon after his arrival here, the Revered Reverend was asked to teach a course about the history of the Protestant Church in China. But the only books he could find on the subject were written by Western missionaries. So he decided to find as much information as he could about 'early Chinese converts'. Using techniques he'd studied in genealogy, he intensively researched local Chinese people's networks and communities. Only after studying Chinese newspapers, official records, archives, wills and cemeteries for over twenty years did he feel he knew enough to write the two books *Chinese Christians: Elites, Middlemen, and the Church in Hong Kong* (1985) and

A Sense of History: Studies in the Social and Urban History of Hong Kong (1995). These books examine the structure and leadership of Chinese society in early colonial Hong Kong.

In 2002, at the age of eighty-four, the Revered Reverend moved to Macau for a full-time job at the Cultural Institute of Macau. Despite failing eyesight he began researching into the social history of the then Portuguese colony. By the end of his life he had accumulated over ten thousand index cards about Hong Kong and Macau. To this day, historians use them to research this region's history.

QUICK FACTS

NAME
  Reverend Carl Smith
GENDER
  Male
BIRTH
  1918
DEATH
  2008
CLAIM TO FAME
  Pastor, teacher and historian

13 A Resourceful Doctor

Courageous Kenneth Uttley
(1901–1972)

K enneth was shy and studious as a boy. He was English and studied medicine at university. In 1929 he came to Hong Kong to join the Medical Service and wrote some important articles on the plague and tuberculosis, the two most common deadly illnesses of the time. He met a nurse and married her. They had three children together and enjoyed a happy life until the Second World War broke out and Hong Kong was occupied by Japanese soldiers.

Dr Uttley sent his wife and children to Australia. Shortly afterwards, he was captured and sent to the prisoner-of-war camp in Stanley. Living conditions inside were appalling. There was barely enough food to survive but trying to escape would almost certainly have resulted in a horrible death.

Instead of despairing, Courageous Kenneth set up a prison hospital and tried to keep his fellow prisoners healthy with the few medicines and instruments he had smuggled into the camp. He recorded details of his daily life by writing tiny words on toilet paper. Writing a proper diary would have been severely punished. One day he described a bee making a nest inside his microscope. Another day he wrote about spotting a shark swimming in the sea.

Sometimes living in such poor conditions caused quarrels. 'The lack of trust between neighbours is a sad reflection on our so-called moral standards,' he wrote. Meanwhile he encouraged prisoners to maintain their good spirits by telling stories, listening to music, singing, and observing wildlife.

At last the war was over and Kenneth was reunited with his family. They chose to stay in Hong Kong, and Kenneth worked for many more years in the Medical Service. In his free time he often went exploring with a former fellow prisoner and they photographed local wildlife together.

QUICK FACTS

NAME
  Kenneth Uttley
GENDER
  Male
BIRTH
  1901
DEATH
  1972
CLAIM TO FAME
  Physician who wrote a diary about Stanley POW camp

Clever Karl Gutzlaff

(1803–1851)

Have you ever wondered who translated the Bible into Chinese? Let me tell you: many people, including a German man called Karl Friedrich August Gutzlaff.

Clever Karl was a nineteenth-century missionary who wanted to spread Christianity to as many Asian people as possible. In 1828 he was sent to Thailand as a Protestant missionary. In 1832 he moved to Korea. But his dearest wish was to spread God's word in China. This wish came true in the early 1830s.

Karl developed a deep knowledge of China from travelling on trading ships that sailed up and down the east coast of the country. In order to appear less foreign, he wore Chinese clothes and false hair when preaching the gospel. He looked so Chinese many people mistook him for one.

Clever Karl was a brilliant linguist who could speak fluent Mandarin as well as Fujianese and Cantonese. His language skills made him very useful to Europeans. For example, he worked as a translator as well as an interpreter for many Hong Kong officials in pre-colonial and colonial times. He became a magistrate too.

Karl lived in Hong Kong for many years. Later in his life he settled in Macau where he married a lady who worked for an organisation called The Promotion of Female Education in the East. It was around this time that he wrote several books about his travels all around Asia.

In 1844 Karl formed the Chinese Christian Union. He trained local Chinese people how to preach and sent them on missions around China. Much to his disappointment, this venture was unsuccessful. He died in Hong Kong in 1851 and is buried at Happy Valley cemetery. His legacy includes a street in Central which is named after him.

QUICK FACTS

NAME

Karl Gutzlaff

GENDER

Male

BIRTH

1803

DEATH

1851

CLAIM TO FAME

Missionary, sinologist, colonial official

Heroic José Rizal

(1861–1896)

In the late nineteenth century very few Filipinos could travel to Hong Kong. The ones that did were often nationalists who opposed Spanish rule of the Philippines. José Rizal lived here for six months in 1891 and became the most famous nationalist of all.

Heroic José was a highly-educated *mestizo*: half Chinese, half Spanish. He spoke Tagalog, Spanish, French and German. He studied in Manila, as well as Spain, France and Germany, gaining several degrees, including a doctorate in ophthalmology. While studying abroad he wrote two books about injustice and corruption in the Philippines, which angered the Spanish authorities very much. When he eventually arrived back home, his family feared for his life and urged him to leave again.

So Heroic José based himself in Hong Kong. He opened a surgery in Central and worked as an eye doctor. He also founded a reformist society called La Liga Filipina. Its aim was to unite Filipinos through educational, cultural and commercial activities. But while travelling to the Philippines to visit his family in 1892 he was arrested and exiled to the south of the country. For four years José lived in Mindanao and worked as a farmer. He also built a school and a local clinic.

In 1896 a rebellion broke out in Manila against the Spanish. José tried to distance himself from it by volunteering to serve as a doctor for sick people in Cuba but he was arrested en route, taken back to the Philippines, put on trial, and accused of treason. Heroic José argued that he was a reformist rather than a revolutionist but the authorities sentenced him to execution by a firing squad.

Many Filipinos were outraged by his death. So when the Spanish were overthrown in 1898, heroic José was hailed the hero of the independence movement.

QUICK FACTS

NAME
  José Rizal
GENDER
  Male
BIRTH
  1861
DEATH
  1896
CLAIM TO FAME
  Philippine nationalist

Savvy Sir Robert Ho Tung

(1862–1956)

S ir Robert Ho Tung spoke fluent Cantonese. He wore black silk gowns, satin slippers and skull caps but had red hair, blue eyes and pale skin. Was he Chinese or Western? It was hard to tell at first sight. The answer is that he was both. Sir Robert was a Eurasian; his father was Dutch and his mother was Chinese.

When Robert was only six years old, his father left Asia and never returned. It was the middle of winter. Robert was hungry and cold.

But he was resilient and clever. He won a place at the best school in Hong Kong and studied very hard. Later he became a *compradore* for a Western company that still operates today: Jardine, Matheson & Company. He brokered deals between Chinese and Western business-men and within a few years became very rich. He also bought property and shares, and became the director of eighteen companies.

During his lifetime Sir Robert gave away vast sums of money to good causes, mainly in the fields of medicine and education. In World War I he bought two aeroplanes for the Royal Flying Corps, as well as ambulances for the Red Cross and St John of Jerusalem Societies. In 1922 he wrote: 'Now I am free from business cares and have enough money to live on, I find it a pleasure to put forth my energy to help my country become strong and peaceful.'

Savvy Sir Robert also campaigned for equal

rights for Chinese. For his efforts he received many medals. He lived to the grand old age of ninety-three and is buried next to his wife in the colonial cemetery at Happy Valley. His rags-to-riches story has been an inspiration for many entrepreneurs and philanthropists.

QUICK FACTS

NAME
  Sir Robert Ho Tung

GENDER
  Male

BIRTH
  1862

DEATH
  1956

CLAIM TO FAME
  Compradore, entrepreneur, philanthropist

Reviled Isogai Rensuke

(1882–1967)

D id you know that between 1941 and 1945 Hong Kong was occupied by the Japanese? Since the 1930s Japan had been aggressively expanding territories under its influence in the hope of creating an East Asian empire.

General Rensuke was sent to China after training at the Imperial Military Academy in Japan. His military record was poor but he had many friends in high places. One of them was Tojo Hideki, the Japanese prime minister, who offered him the opportunity to work in Hong Kong. General Rensuke thus became the territory's first and only Japanese governor.

Governer-General Rensuke was ordered to establish Hong Kong as a military base from where the Japanese army could launch attacks on other Asian countries. He put strict control on local people's movements and business activities, arresting and imprisoning many Hongkongers. He forced everyone to use the Japanese yen instead of Hong Kong dollars and commanded his soldiers to confiscate anything that could be resold. As a result, Hongkongers become poorer and poorer, hungrier and hungrier. Rather than organise food for them, Rensuke deported them to other countries. Many people died at sea.

As the years passed, Reviled Rensuke was seen around Hong Kong less and less. He lived in Repulse Bay where he practised calligraphy and enjoyed the croaking of bullfrogs. It's possible he didn't know what terrible cruelties his soldiers were committing around the territory.

When the war ended, he was captured, tried and imprisoned for life. But when sent back to Japan to serve his sentence, he was released after only five years. Resilient Rensuke then lived a quiet life. 1964 was the last time he was seen in public, in Tokyo, at the Olympic Games.

QUICK FACTS

NAME
Isogai Rensuke
GENDER
Male
BIRTH
1882
DEATH
1967
CLAIM TO FAME
Japanese Governor-General of Hong Kong

18   A Saver of Lives

Crafty Chan Chak

(1894–1949)

Question: why did a one-legged Chinese admiral and sixty-two British officers swim from Aberdeen to Ap Lei Chau on Christmas Day in 1941? Answer: to get to the other side! They were under heavy fire from Japanese soldiers who were invading Hong Kong.

At that time, Admiral Chan was a member of the Chinese Nationalist government and the most senior Mainland official in Hong Kong. Since 1938 he had been working as a secret agent to help the British prepare for a possible

Japanese attack. In the rush and confusion of the invasion, Admiral Chan didn't have time to pick up his wooden leg. It was stuffed with money he'd planned to pay people along the way in the event of a retreat.

Admiral Chan was a short man in weak health. While swimming he was shot in the wrist by one of the hundreds of bullets the Japanese were firing. But high-speed motor boats were lying in wait on Ap Lei Chau and Crafty Admiral Chan took charge of all the men. Even without his wooden leg, he succeeded in getting the English officers over the border to China. Then, with his language skills and knowledge of the local landscape, he led a long march across the countryside into safe territory.

After being treated for his shattered wrist and a stomach ulcer, Admiral Chan continued to work for the resistance in occupied Hong

Kong. For example, in 1943, he managed to sneak two thousand Chinese soldiers into the territory to fight the Japanese. After the war, the British awarded him a KBE (Knight of the British Empire). They also arranged for woodworkers in India to carve him a beautiful new leg.

From August 1945 Admiral Chan took office in China as Guangzhou's first post-war mayor. He worked tirelessly on rebuilding the city. But sadly he died of overwork when he was only fifty-six years old.

QUICK FACTS

NAME
  Chan Chak
GENDER
  Male
BIRTH
  1894
DEATH
  1949
CLAIM TO FAME
  Naval officer and hero

19 A Generous Billionaire

Loaded Loke Yew

(1846–1917)

I wonder how many of you will study at the University of Hong Kong (HKU) one day. If you do you'll probably attend a ceremony at Loke Yew Hall in the university's main building. This hall is named after a Chinese businessman who had no education himself.

Loke Yew was born into a peasant family in Guangdong and orphaned at a very early age. In 1858 when he was only twelve, he went to Singapore as a 'free immigrant' and worked as a shop assistant for four years.

Why did the first Resident-General of British Malaya once declare that Loke Yew was 'the most enterprising Chinese I know'? It was because of Loke Yew's incredible hard work and shrewd eye for business. First he saved up enough money to open his own shop. Then, when mining rights to Chinese migrants were auctioned in Malaysia, he bought many. Soon he was operating twelve tin mines. He expanded his business quickly by importing workers from Hong Kong.

By the 1890s Loke Yew had a vast business empire in the areas of mining, gambling, pawn-broking, opium, rubber and rice. He also had interests in cars, steamships and engineering. With his profits, he bought real estate in Kuala Lumpur and Singapore, where a street is still named after him.

Loke Yew's incredible wealth brought him respect in Chinese communities all over Southeast Asia. He garnered even more admiration by his philanthropy, especially in the area of education. Why is HKU's main hall named after him? Because in 1911 he gave a large donation towards its construction. Four years later he offered the university an additional $500,000 interest-free loan. The university awarded him an honorary doctorate in recognition of his extraordinary generosity.

QUICK FACTS

NAME

Loke Yew

GENDER

Male

BIRTH

1846

DEATH

1917

CLAIM TO FAME

Entrepreneur and philanthropist

Doomed Duanzong
(1268–1278)
Brother Bing Di
(1272–1279)

Did you know that one Southern Song dynasty Emperor died in Hong Kong and another was crowned? They were half-brothers, little boys, sons of Emperor Duzong. Why were they here when their capital city was present-day Hangzhou in Zhejiang? They had fled from a horde of Mongols who wanted to seize control.

The boys were taken by boat from China by faithful courtiers and landed somewhere in Kowloon. At that time Kowloon wasn't yet called Kowloon (literally 'nine dragons'). Apparently the local villagers named it so in honour of the imperial entourage's arrival, counting the Emperor as one of the dragons (mountain peaks).

According to history, the elder boy was crowned Emperor Duanzong near Mui Wo on Lantau Island in the summer of 1277. There is a plaque near the ferry pier to commemorate this event. Afterwards the Emperor and his entourage stayed in present-day Tsuen Wan. But alas, after only two months, they received news that Mongols were sailing down the coast with the intent to kill them.

Doomed Duanzong, his brother and their courtiers set out to sea. Records report that they struck a typhoon in the Pearl River Delta, the Emperor nearly drowned, and later died of his injuries. Where he is buried remains a mystery to this day.

A few months later, in May 1278, his half-brother Bing Di, aged seven, was crowned Emperor. Tragically, he reigned for less than a year because the Mongols attacked. There was a big naval battle in the Pearl River Delta in March 1279 and the Mongols won. It's reported that Lu Xiufu, the most loyal of the boys' ministers, carried Bing Di on his back and jumped into the sea, thereby ending the Song dynasty. The historical relic Sung Wong Toi in Kowloon City commemorates this.

QUICK FACTS

NAME

Doomed Duanzong and Brother Bing Di

GENDER

Male

BIRTH

1268, 1272

DEATH

1278, 1279

CLAIM TO FAME

Chinese emperors

Cunning Cheung Po Tsai
(1786–1822)

Don't think pirates are jolly men who swing from masts and dance jigs. Nineteenth-century Hong Kong pirates were murderers, kidnappers and scavengers. Working in gangs, they demanded protection money from fishermen, seized booty from local villagers and raided the heavily-laden merchant ships sailing up and down the Pearl River from Canton to Hong Kong.

Cheung Po Tsai was a fisherman's son. At the age of fifteen, while fishing, he was kidnapped by the leader of the most powerful gang of them all – Zheng Yi of the Red Banner fleet. Po Tsai was quickly trained in the art of piracy and was soon causing trouble on the waterways. His gang frequently fought with the second-most powerful gang, the Black Banner fleet. So fearless was Po Tsai that when Zheng Yi was killed, the Red Banner pirates elected him unanimously as their new leader.

At the height of his power, Cunning Cheung controlled hundreds of ships and seventeen thousand men. Legend has it that the famous cave you can visit on Cheung Chau island used to be stuffed to the top with his treasure.

But in 1809 the Chinese Emperor Jiaqing took action. He appointed a brave man called Bai Ling as the governor-general of Guangdong. Bai Ling cut off the food supply to the pirates and formed a neighbourhood reporting system called *baojia* to spy on them. He also commissioned local armies and built fortifications from where soldiers could bombard them with cannon balls.

In October of that year a big battle was fought between the Red Banners and a Chinese government fleet near Chep Lap Kok. Cunning Cheung managed to escape but the government forces smashed his fleet and he later was forced to surrender. Interestingly, Emperor Jiaqing later pardoned him, offered him a job in the Chinese navy and ordered him to help eliminate other pirate gangs!

QUICK FACTS

NAME
  Cheung Po Tsai
GENDER
  Male
BIRTH
  1786
DEATH
  1822
CLAIM TO FAME
  Pirate

Hard-working Ho Kai

(1859–1914)

Ho Kai succeeded by unstinting hard work. Born in Hong Kong and educated in England, he was trained as both a doctor and a lawyer. During his lifetime he set up many businesses, fathered seventeen children and was a key player in Hong Kong's political scene.

On Ho Kai's return from England, he opened a doctor's clinic. But Chinese people weren't willing to pay for Western medicine. So he worked as a barrister instead. He invested in land and property too. Hong Kong's old airport at Kai Tak was named after him because it was built on his land.

Ho Kai never stopped promoting the medical profession to the Chinese community. In his legal work he often represented the poorest of the poor who lived in crowded tenements with little space, light or ventilation. In 1890 Ho Kai opposed a government proposal to improve inmates' welfare by providing separate cells in prisons. That's because he thought some people may deliberately commit crimes to get some privacy! In 1894 when local workers and boatmen went on strike he defended them for free. In 1908 he campaigned for the rights of three thousand rickshaw pullers.

In later years, Hard-working Ho became more socially active. He was a member of the Legislative Council and board member of all of

Hong Kong's main hospitals. He was also a member of the Sanitary Board and the Public Works Committee. Working to promote Hong Kong as a commercial and political model for China, he wrote a six-volume series of books on social reform.

Hard-working Ho was declared bankrupt after his death. Some say it was because he was involved in too many activities. Others say it was because his business partners tricked him. But he had made so many positive changes to Hong Kong society that the colonial government offered his family a burial plot in Happy Valley Cemetery.

QUICK FACTS

NAME
  Ho Kai
GENDER
  Male
BIRTH
  1859
DEATH
  1914
CLAIM TO FAME
  Chinese hero – barrister, physician, businessman

Showy Sun Ma Sze-tsang

(1916–1997)

Imagine a world without smartphones or computers, television or radio. That's what Hong Kong was like in the 1930s, the time when Cantonese opera was the most popular form of entertainment. And if you'd gone to one, you may have had the good fortune to see the Chinese opera star Sun Ma Sze-tsang performing.

Sun Ma's real family name was Tang. He was born in Guangdong province. When his parents' marriage broke up, his father brought him to Hong Kong and remarried. His stepmother kicked him out of the family home a year later. Master Tang was only eight years old. But luckily he was recruited by a local opera troupe where his talent for acting and his beautiful voice were quickly recognised. Within a few years, he'd been renamed Sun Ma after the opera superstar Ma Sze-tsang.

Sun Ma sang in professional shows from a very young age. While only a teenager, he formed his own troupe, writing, directing and starring in many popular productions. He also performed Peking opera. From the mid-1930s, when silent movies with voiceovers became popular ('talking pictures'), Sun Ma started making his own. Notably he sang in all his movies and operas, whether comedy or tragedy, contemporary or costumed.

The movie industry came to a standstill during the Japanese occupation (1941–1945).

But by the 1950s Sun Ma was working again. In 1963 he established the Wing Cheung Film Company. Over his lifetime he appeared in over two hundred films and accumulated a personal fortune of over one billion dollars.

Every year, from 1950 to 1994, Showy Sun Ma performed at the annual Tung Wah Hospital Charity Show. This earned him the nickname 'Charity Opera King'. He was awarded an honorary doctorate by Oxford University in 1977 and an MBA in 1978.

QUICK FACTS

NAME
  Sun Ma Sze-tsang
GENDER
  Male
BIRTH
  1916
DEATH
  1997
CLAIM TO FAME
  Cantonese opera singer and film actor

Shrewd Sir
Murray MacLehose
(1917–2000)

Have you heard of the MacLehose Trail?
Named after Sir Murray, the twenty-fifth governor of Hong Kong, it is a demanding hundred-kilometre hike across the highest mountains of the New Territories. You need sturdy legs and a few free days to walk from the beginning to the end!

Sir Murray governed Hong Kong from 1971 to 1982. His was nicknamed 'Big Mac', not after a beef burger, but because he was tall, energetic and ambitious. His policies produced many positive changes in Hong Kong. For example, he made it compulsory for all children to attend primary school. He also set up a social welfare programme and established country parks. In 1972 he masterminded a massive 'Ten-Year Housing Scheme' to provide homes for the poor. In 1974 he tried to stop corruption by establishing the 'Independent Commission Against Corruption (ICAC)'. As a result a cultural change took place here: Hongkongers came to regard corruption as unacceptable and felt proud of their success in eliminating it.

Sir Murray was well liked by the general public. He would often be seen around town wearing ordinary clothes and listening to people's views. He handled many crises. For example, when a landslide killed eighteen people at the Sau Mau Ping housing estate in 1976, he studied why it happened and hired top engineers to improve slopes all over Hong Kong.

Shrewd Sir Murray is famous for starting negotiations with China about Hong Kong's future. He changed the word 'colony' to 'territory', and the position of 'colonial secretary' to 'chief secretary'. In 1981, when the expiry of the lease for the New Territories was only sixteen years away, he discussed Hong Kong's future with Deng Xiaoping in Beijing. It's recorded that the chairman clearly told him that China wanted Hong Kong back.

QUICK FACTS

NAME
  Sir Murray MacLehose
GENDER
  Male
BIRTH
  1917
DEATH
  2000
CLAIM TO FAME
  25th governor of Hong Kong

Scholarly Szeto Wah

(1931–2011)

Have you ever heard your parents talking about Uncle Wah? If so, they mean Szeto Wah, the political activist who campaigned for democracy in Hong Kong and China. When he died of cancer in 2011 there was an outpouring of grief from many people in Hong Kong society.

Uncle Wah came from a poor family. His father worked in a shipyard. When Japanese bombed Hong Kong, his family escaped to Guangdong where young Wah saw much death and destruction. This sad experience made him dedicate his life to building a strong and prosperous China.

Uncle Wah was a teacher by profession. He studied at Queen's College and Grantham College of Education where he worked for nine years, later becoming its headmaster. He founded a union for teachers – the Professional Teachers' Union – and in 1973 organised a teachers' strike in order to protest against a government decision to cut teachers' pay. In 1978 he campaigned for Chinese language teaching in Hong Kong secondary schools. In 1982 he led protests after the Japanese government was reported to have changed school textbooks to play down war atrocities against China committed in the 1930s and 1940s.

Uncle Wah was also a politician. In 1990 he co-founded the United Democrats of Hong

Kong which became one of the largest parties in the Legislative Council. In preparation for the handover of Hong Kong back to China in 1997, he was appointed by the Chinese government to help draw up the Basic Law.

Scholarly Uncle Wah was proud to be Chinese. He was skilled at calligraphy and had a great love for Chinese history and culture. He had a warm personality and high integrity but never married or had children. Even his political opponents liked and respected him. In 1997 the famous American magazine *Time* named him one of 'The 25 Most Influential People in the New Hong Kong'.

QUICK FACTS

NAME

Szeto Wah

GENDER

Male

BIRTH

1931

DEATH

2011

CLAIM TO FAME

Unionist and political activist

Hardy Ho A-mei

(1838–1901)

A-mei was an orphan but received an excellent education at a free Anglo-Chinese school in Central. His first business venture was to send Chinese 'coolies' to Australia where they worked in goldmines. Hardy Ho fought hard to protect their rights. He married an Englishwoman in Australia and she bore him two children.

Ho returned to Hong Kong ten years later and continued his entrepreneurial work. He established the first Chinese-owned insurance company and developed the mining industry, here and on the Mainland. Have you ever visited the silver mine in Mui Wo on Lantau Island? It was co-owned by Ho A-mei. Unfortunately the quality of the silver was so poor it was closed after only a few years' operation. It has since become a popular tourist attraction.

Mr Ho also became a community leader, often campaigning against what he considered to be discrimination in the colony. For example in 1885, while chairman of the Tung Wah Hospital, he broke the law prohibiting direct communication between local residents and Mainland Chinese officials by receiving a special scroll from the Chinese Emperor. A year later, in 1886, he organised a public meeting for the abolition of the regulations which required Chinese residents who went outdoors after dark to carry passes and lights.

Hardy Ho became the chairman of the first

Chinese Chamber of Commerce. In defiance of the British colonial government he showed his loyalty to China by wearing Qing dynasty robes and inviting imperial mandarins to attend meetings. He also lobbied hard for the establishment of a Chinese consul in Hong Kong.

After years of active service and business deals, Mr Ho built up many good contacts in China. In 1898 he decided to close his Hong Kong companies and retire to Canton, present-day Guangzhou. Little is known about his life after then but he died two years later.

QUICK FACTS

NAME

Ho A-mei

GENDER

Male

BIRTH

1838

DEATH

1901

CLAIM TO FAME

Entrepreneur, community leader

Single-minded
Sir Matthew Nathan
(1862–1939)

Have you ever walked along Nathan Road in Kowloon? Did you do some shopping and enjoy the long stretch of colourful neon lights? If so, you have Sir Matthew Nathan to thank.

When Sir Matthew became the thirteenth Hong Kong governor in 1906, Kowloon was still a swampy backwater, dark and dangerous at nights, and a criminals' refuge.

But Hong Kong's population was growing fast and food to feed all the people couldn't be shipped in quickly enough. Why not build a road from Tsim Sha Tsui to the New Territories? thought Sir Matthew. That would enable Hongkongers to grow their own food and transport it into the city. And so Sir Matthew – an ex-military officer, a trained engineer with experience of building roads in other British colonies – proposed the construction of Nathan Road.

Too expensive, said some. Too long, said others. Many people were totally against his idea and named the project 'Nathan's Folly'. But single-minded Sir Matthew ignored them. He planned ahead and ordered the building materials anyway.

Setting up the Kowloon–Canton Railway was another very unpopular project of his. Although the Hong Kong Chamber of Commerce promoted it, the Chinese government protested, calling Sir Matthew all kinds of unpleasant names. But the governor raised the money himself and organised the building of the railway anyway.

Sadly, in 1906, Sir Matthew fell off a horse, bumped his head rather badly and had to leave Hong Kong for medical treatment. He later continued his brilliant career with government posts in present-day South Africa, Sri Lanka, United Kingdom and Australia. Here is a list of his titles: CMG, KCMG, GCMG. You can check what they mean on Google.

During his long career in public service Sir Matthew travelled widely. But he is quoted as saying that his days in Hong Kong were the happiest of his life.

QUICK FACTS

NAME

Sir Matthew Nathan

GENDER

Male

BIRTH

1862

DEATH

1939

CLAIM TO FAME

Built Nathan Road and the Kowloon–Canton Railway

Glorious Gloria
D'Almada Barretto
(1916–2007)

G loria was an adventurous child. Brought up in Fan Ling surrounded by farmers, fields and buffaloes, she would gallop her horse beside the little-used Kowloon–Canton Railway, or stay up late to watch fireflies dancing in the bushes. Gloria loved the countryside so much she taught herself the names of all Hong Kong's flowers and trees.

Gloria's studies temporarily stopped in the 1940s while the territory was occupied by the Japanese. There was a prisoner-of-war camp near where she lived. Risking her life, she smuggled news about the war into the camp on the lids of jam jars.

After the war she worked as a botanist. In her free time, she explored many relatively remote parts of Hong Kong and found many previously unknown species of orchids. Orchids would become her specialty. Do you know why she could tell the difference between a *Bulbophyllum tseanum* and a *Cheiostylis clibborndyeri?* Because she had discovered and named them herself!

In the 1980s Gloria was invited to Guangdong to help the Chinese government classify and document wild orchids on the mainland. She also campaigned to keep Tsim Sha Tsui's famous Kowloon–Canton Railway terminus clock tower. Without her objections the tower would probably not be standing today.

Glorious Gloria wrote the best book ever

on Hong Kong orchids. It's called *Wild Orchids of Hong Kong*. You can see samples of the orchids she found and identified in a garden named after her at Kadoorie Farm where she worked until she was eighty-seven years old. It is largely through her efforts that the farm has become Hong Kong's conservation centre of biodiversity. As well as Gloria's orchids, you can also see organic farming, botanical gardens, native forest, and rare rescued animals. It's well worth a trip.

QUICK FACTS

NAME

Gloria d'Almada Barretto

GENDER

Female

BIRTH

1916

DEATH

2007

CLAIM TO FAME

Botanist and pioneer of the conservation of natural habitat

The Awe-inspiring Aw Brothers

Aw Boon Haw (1882–1954)

Aw Boon Par (1884–1944)

Has anyone told you they love Tiger Balm? It's an ointment that relaxes muscles and nerves. You can pop it in your pocket for easy use. I'm sure you'd recognise its distinctive odour. The brothers Aw Boon Haw and Aw Boon Par are famous for making Tiger Balm ointment a household name.

Nicknamed 'Tiger' and 'Leopard', the brothers were brought up in Burma (present-day Myanmar) where their father owned a Chinese medicine shop. Exactly who created

Tiger Balm ointment remains a secret between them but when their father died, the brothers worked tirelessly to promote it. First they travelled across Asia to get ideas about how to make the ointment seem attractive. Then they designed a tin box, colouring it bright red and adding a leaping tiger on the lid.

Between 1929 and 1951 the Awe-inspiring Aw brothers founded seventeen Chinese- and English-language newspapers in Hong Kong, China and Southeast Asia. Can you guess why they built a publishing empire? In order to promote Tiger Balm. At that time there were many similar products on the market and advertising in newspapers was the best way to let as many people as possible know about Tiger Balm. Their strategy worked. Tiger Balm is still the best known ointment of its kind in the world.

The Aw brothers also became rich from

investing in banking, property and rubber companies. To share their wealth with Hong Kong people they set up a large amusement park in Tai Hang on Hong Kong Island where children could play, adults could rest, and history lovers could admire statues and scenes from ancient Chinese stories. Maybe your parents visited the park when they were young.

QUICK FACTS

NAME
  Aw Boon Haw and Aw Boon Par
GENDER
  Males
BIRTH
  1882, 1884
DEATH
  1954, 1944
CLAIM TO FAME
  Manufactured Tiger Balm and founded a publishing corporation

The Successful Sassoon Family

Imagine feeling discriminated against in your home country because of your religious beliefs. That happened to many Jewish people, including members of the Sassoon family, who moved from Iraq to India and East Asia to escape persecution.

Based in present-day Mumbai, David Sassoon formed an international trading company by sending his eight sons to establish branch offices all over the world, including Hong Kong. The family exported silk and tea from China and imported metals, cotton and opium. Many companies were involved in the opium business in the early colonial days of Hong Kong. Opium grew in India where the Sassoon brothers' boats stopped on their way to Asia. Selling this highly-addictive drug to Chinese people generated staggering profits for them.

But David and his sons were religious. They felt guilty about being in the drugs business. So over the years they invested more in property, shipping and banking. One son was a founding member of the Hongkong and Shanghai Bank. Another was a member of the Legislative Council. All of them donated generously to good causes. This included gifting a large piece of land in Happy Valley for a Jewish cemetery. To this day, Jewish people can be buried there.

From the 1930s the successful Sassoon

brothers sold their business interests in Hong Kong and invested more in Shanghai. But their legacy here remains: Sassoon Road in Pok Fu Lam, and a beautiful place of worship called Ohel Leah Synagogue in Mid-Levels. This synagogue is a meeting place for the thousands of Jewish people who still live here. There's also a Jewish Community Centre which offers interesting cultural and musical events. Some of these events are open to the public. So if you want to know the difference between a tower and a Torah, a bar and a *bar mitzvah*, do attend them some time.

QUICK FACTS

NAME

Sassoon family

GENDER

Males

BIRTH

Late 19th century onwards

DEATH

NA

CLAIM TO FAME

Traders, industrialists, bankers and philanthropists

Index of Chinese Names

Chinese names are written in traditional Chinese characters, with simplified Chinese characters in brackets.

29. The Inventors of Tiger Balm

The Awe-inspiring Aw Brothers

Aw Boon Haw 胡文虎（胡文虎）

Aw Boon Par 胡文豹（胡文豹）